Princess Kaguya

from the moon

Based on "Taketori Monogatari"

Illustrated by

Eiko Jasmine

First published in the United Kingdom 2008
By Perfect Publishers Ltd

Princess Kaguya

Printed in England by Lightning Source UK Ltd.

ISBN 978-1-905399-34-5

Perfect Publishers Ltd
23 Maitland Avenue
Cambridge
CB4 1TA
England

www.perfectpublishers.co.uk

Forewords

"Taketori Monogatari," literally translated "The Tale of the Bamboo Cutter" is familiar to the Japanese people by the title " Kaguya Hime." It is considered the oldest story in Japanese literature born around the 10th century. It was passed down by the word of mouth so the exact author is unknown. However the story is extremely well known and is part of the core curriculum of the junior-high level of Japanese literature. The students learn to read and understand the ancient Japanese literature and seek depth in their poetic language that was used in the aristocratic society. The story reflects the "romance" aspect of the aristocrats in those times, and how they express their love with beautiful "songs" they wrote to each other. It is even referred as being the "ancestor of all romances" in a classic Japanese literature, "The Tale of Genji."

Since moving to England from Japan, I continued my profession as a teacher at Japanese schools in UK. Japanese businessmen are often sent abroad to the UK to work temporarily, and they usually bring their families with them. The children from these families are sent to Japanese schools in UK to be taught the Japanese curriculum on top of the English curriculum. I noticed that whilst there is an interest in Japanese culture especially among the younger generations in England, there is lack of access to knowledge of the culture. There is a wealth of Japanese literature which unfortunately is rarely translated into English. I feel that in order to understand Japanese culture, an appreciation of ancient Japanese life is needed. Through this book, I hope to provide some insight into Japanese literature and culture by telling the story of 'Princess Kaguya' in the form of the Manga style which is very popular in Japan. I hope that this book will be enjoyed and stimulate further interest in Japanese literature and culture.

Dedication

With grateful thanks to eternal friends and my family

Especially

To my son, Shunsuke and my daughter, Yuki who supported me throughout this project

Once upon a time...

there was an old man,
called ' TAKETORI-no-OKINA$_2$.'
His name was 'SANUKI-no-MIYATSUKO.'

He had been to the grove to
cut bamboo. He used
the bamboo to make things .

1

One day,
he noticed a bamboo shining, close to the root.

What ?!

God heavens!
How tiny!
How beautiful!

He cut the shining bamboo
slowly and cautiously.

Inside was a beautiful girl,
less than 10cm tall.

2

Okina carefully carried the girl home.

What happened, Okina?

Ouna₃ was so surprised.

Okina told his wife 'Ouna' about the happening in the grove. As they did not have any children they decided to look after her.

Praise be! Our dreams have at last come true.

Beautiful, isn't she? Her clothes look so worthy. Do you think maybe God gave her to us?

From the next day onwards, Okina continued to
find treasures when he cut the bamboo.

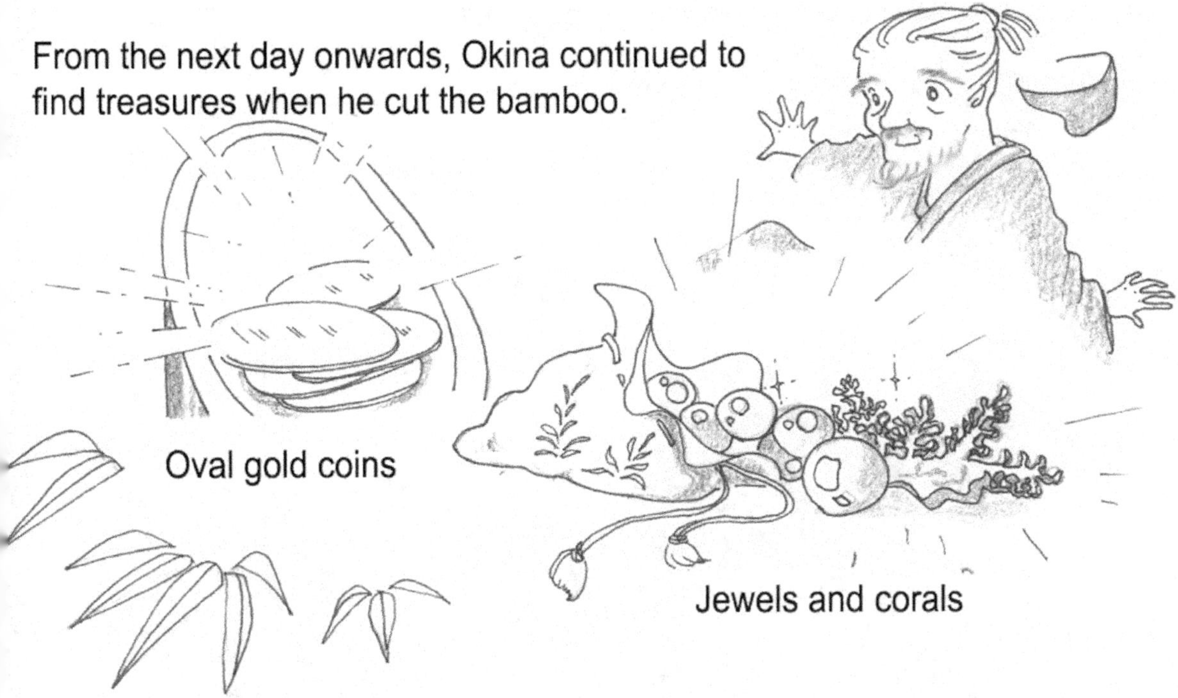

Oval gold coins

Jewels and corals

Okina and Ouna became rich.
They were able to have a splendid palatial house with servants.

Okina and Ouna loved the girl very much.
She grew and grew day by day.
She knew the scent of flowers, the touch of
life and the feeling of the winds.

5

3 months passed.
The girl grew into a beautiful
lady-unearthly!

Okina and Ouna asked someone
to name her. She was named
NAYOTAKE-no-KAGUYA HIME.

She was beautifully
shining, it was like
full moon light.

Is the rumor true? Did you see the girl?

I've just heard of it.

We should introduce Kaguya to the public. She was given nice name. What do you think?

Over the next 3 days, they invited people to their home and celebrated.

6

Crowds of people gathered at Okina's house most days to
try to peep at Kaguya from dawn to dusk.

One morning, a wealthy looking man visited Okina's house
accompanied by servants.

Who is
he?

Excuse us,
excuse us.

Kuramochi-no-Miko[4]

8

I am Kuramochi.
Would you lift the blinds up for me, please?

I do not see anyone.
Would you leave me, please.

How's Kaguya? She didn't see him. He was of high birth, wasn't he? What's wrong?

It's not like that, I think. But now is a good time to find a man for her.

Mother! Father!

I found a lovely phrase from a Chinese poem ....

Kaguya pretends not to hear...

Princess Kaguya was so clever, so gentle and so beautiful.
However, Okina and Ouna were anxious for her future.

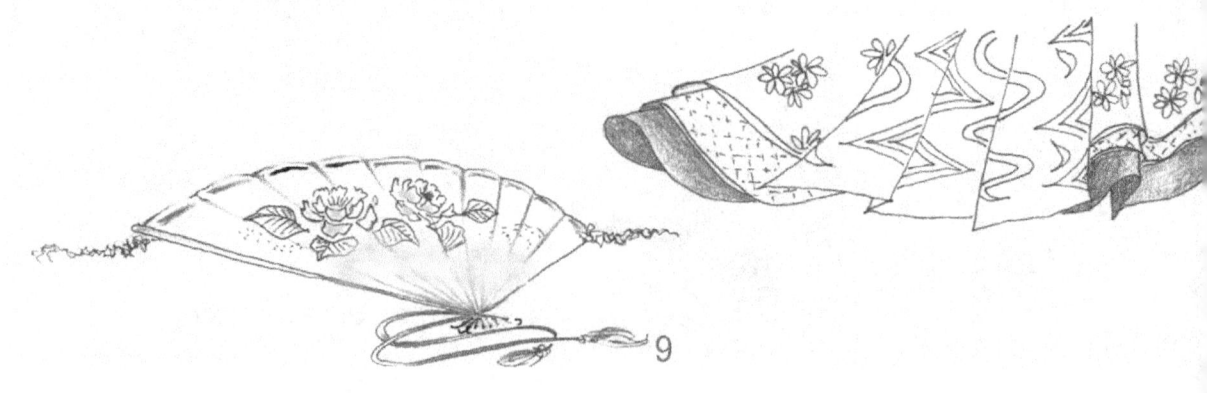

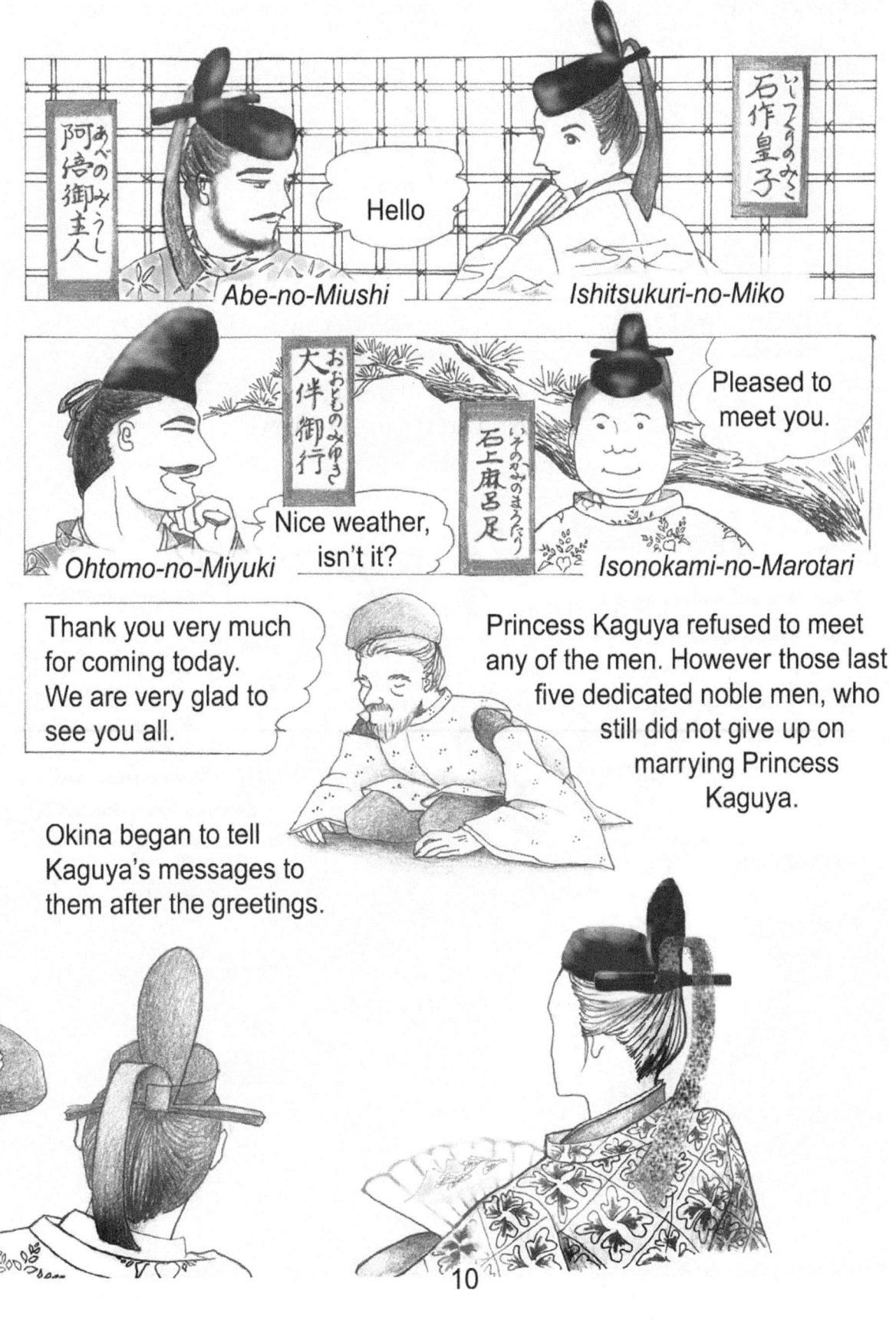

Hello

Abe-no-Miushi

Ishitsukuri-no-Miko

Pleased to meet you.

Nice weather, isn't it?

Ohtomo-no-Miyuki

Isonokami-no-Marotari

Thank you very much for coming today. We are very glad to see you all.

Princess Kaguya refused to meet any of the men. However those last five dedicated noble men, who still did not give up on marrying Princess Kaguya.

Okina began to tell Kaguya's messages to them after the greetings.

10

"Few days ago, my wife and I talked to Kaguya."

Kaguya, usually a woman marries a man.

You are no exception. You should choose one of the five men.

Then she said,
" If I have to marry someone, I will do. But the man should complete a task for me. He should bring me the following."

HORAI-no-TAMA-no-EDA$_6$?

HOTOKE-no-MIISHI-no-HACHI$_7$?

RYU-no-KUBI-no-TAMA$_9$?

TSUBAKURAME-no-KOYASUGAI$_8$?

"Kaguya promised that if any of the men brought her treasure back, she would agree to marry the man."
Okina concluded politely.

HINEZUMI-no-KAWAGINU$_{10}$?

11

After listening to Kaguya's requests, the five noble
men pondered the tasks. It was like catching
a cloud for them.
They had heard of such treasures in ancient
legends, but none of them knew where to find
them.

Ishitsukuri-no-Miko was to look for a shallow
virsion of Buddha's bowl.

Abe-no-Miushi had to think of an animal which
he had never seen before.

Isonokami-no-Marotari was chuckling to himself
because a swallow's nest would be found easily.

Ohtomo-no-Miyuki would put too much trust
in his bravery and power.

Kuramochi-no-Miko was smiling because
he thought that only he would be able to return
successfully.

~The case of Ishitsukuri-no-Miko

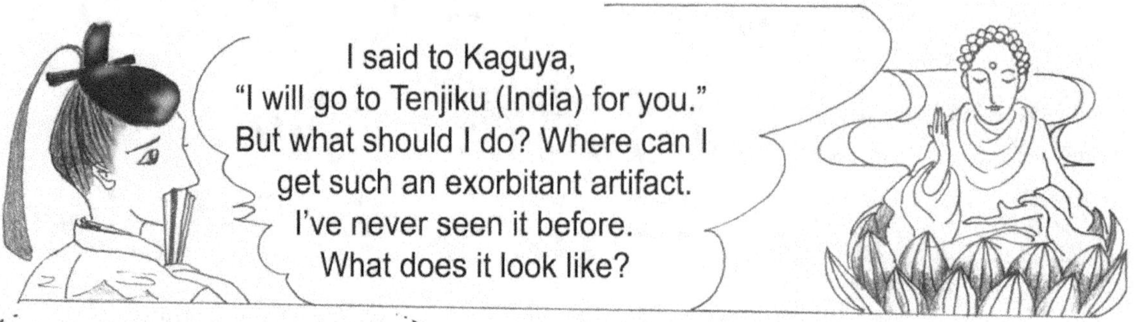

I said to Kaguya,
"I will go to Tenjiku (India) for you."
But what should I do? Where can I
get such an exorbitant artifact.
I've never seen it before.
What does it look like?

I will hide for a while to make
her think that I really went,
but there is no way I am going
that far.

Prepare for a
long journey.
Hurry up!

Ishitsukuri-no-Miko set off with
his servants, pretending to go to
Tenjiku to get the bowl.

Yes,
Sir!

13

Three years passed. He carefully picked the time and a place near
an abandoned temple.He found an old bowl there.

This is old enough to look authentic.
It just needs a polish.
I shall wrap it with silk cloth,
then put it in a box.
That it!

crumbling

Who's going to polish that dirty thing?

Looks quite dirty, but
HOTOKE-no-MIISHI-no-HACHI...

Ishitsukuri-no-Miko presented the bowl to Kaguya as the genuine Buddha's bowl from Indea with the unusual flower.

This bowl was shiny and beautiful but it has lost its sheen in front of you, Princess Kaguya.

Although he tried to fool Princess Kaguya with dramatic stories about his journey to find the bowl, she could see through his lies.

I thought no one would find out the truth, but at a first glance, she knew that the bowl was not genuine.

As soon as Ishitsukuri-no-Miko left Okina's house, the bowl turned into stones.

15

~The case of Abe-no-Miushi~

Hinezumi lives in the volcano, I've heard.

Hinezumi? Clothes?

Sir,

We've heard that clothing made with Hinezumi cannot burn, but we haven't seen it before. What shall we do?

Abe-no-Miushi wrote a letter to a Chinese trader.
"If you have any clothing made with Hinezumi fur, could you please send it to me. I am willing to pay any price for it."

He sent a servant to deliver the letter and money to the trader.

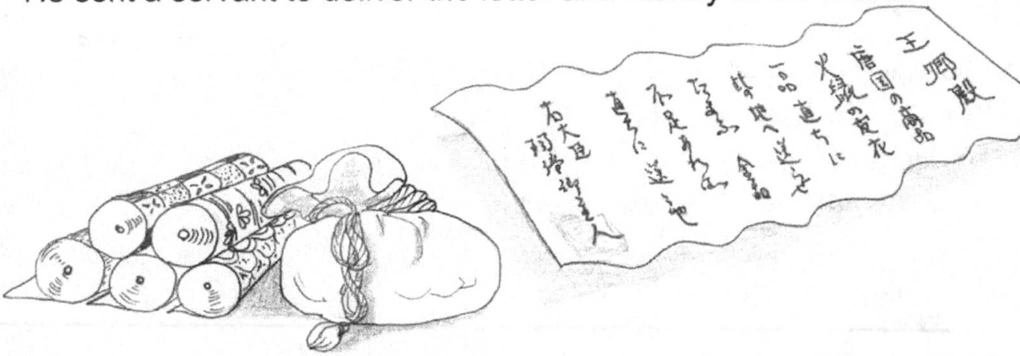

As he was so rich he did not mind how much he had to pay for the clothing. He had to wait two years before he recieved it.

16

Two years later...

This is a jacket made with the fur of Hinezumi. It came from Tenjiku.

Well done!

I have been told that it will not burn. Apparently it's even more beautiful when it is put through a fire.

Is it true?

Since I had to work harder than expected to get it, could you pay me more?

No problem!

Abe-no-Miushi placed the alleged HINEZUMI-no-KAWAGIMU jacket into a gorgeous, jewelled box. He was sure that Princess Kaguya would like it, so he dressed up for the evening.

Although I paid a lot of money, I don't mind - if she is going to be pleased with it. That jacket is truely splendid. I will be able to see the face of Princess Kaguya very soon.

17

The only thing connecting me to you is this HINEZUMI-no-KAWAGINU. My love for you is so strong that my emotions have turned to tears which dampened my sleeves every night. However, if it is possible to see your smile, none of the loneliness would matter.....

We'll know whether it's the real thing or not when we put it into the fire.

A braizier was brought in and a fire was made using charcoal before the jacket was placed into the flames.

What a terrible waste to do such a thing!

Far from becoming more beautiful, it quickly turned to ash.

Abe-no-Miushi looked terribly pale. It was told that he could not eat anything for a while.

18

~The case of **Isonokami-no-Marotari**~

Sir!
Are you alright?

Isonokami-no-Marotari fell head first.
He could not get up for a while after that.

The only thing he had managed to grab was
a handful of dung!

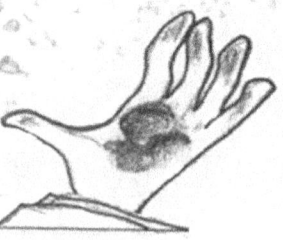

~The case of Ohtomo-no-Miyuki~

What's happening?

One day, all employees were called in a room.

Maybe one of us has an award.

Did we do something wrong?

I'm setting a challenge for all of you. I want the jewel on the dragon's neck.

I'll reward with anything if any of you bring the jewel to me.

Understood?

What should I do? I can't kill a dragon.

It's too dangerous. We'll be given retribution.

The dragon was believed to be the Incarnated spirit of God.

The dragon's jewel changes colour from black to white, yellow, blue and red, which controls Mother Nature.

Whilst Ohtomo-no-Miyuki was waiting for the dragon's jewel, he built a house for Princess Kaguya.

A few months later...

Ohtomo-no-Miyuki had not received any news about the jewel.

What are they doing? I'm starting to get impatient. Prepare for a journey!

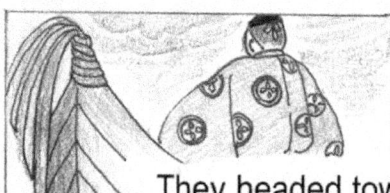

Sir! It's going to rain. You'd better go back.

They headed towards the sea where the dragon was known to live.

I don't mind. It doesn't look so bad.

Suddenly, lightning struck and large waves crashed into the boat. They were in the middle of a violent storm.

23

He prayed for the storm to stop.
He apologised for his arrogance and
foolishness to the God.
And he asked for his employees' lives
to be spared-no one had come back from
the jewel hunting.

The storm has gone.

The sea became calm.

It's calm at last.
We can go back now.

The new house was
destroyed by the storm.

Only Ohtomo-no-Miyuki had been in bed for a
while with terrible seasickness and swollen
eyelids.

Employees had
come back safely and
got back to work.

I guess, it's much better
to have a cup of rice wine
than to fall in love with
someone who is out of
my league.

24

~The case of Kuramochi-no-Miko~

Have a safe journey, Sir!

Kuramochi-no-Miko had set off to Mt.HORAI to find TAMA-no-EDA with his servants.
'HORAI' was told that it was an island in the east .

He got on a boat to pretend to go to the island.

All preparations are completed. Kaguya would be mine in three years time.

Kuramochi-no-Miko planned very carefully. He did not go to HORAI. He hid with his servants in a secure house with high fences.

Over the next three years, I want you to make a beautiful branch. Please, don't tell anyone about this place.

You can trust us!

Six specialists of beautiful craftwork began to make TAMA-no-EDA from many precious and expensive materials.

They worked day in and day out, each craftsman undertaking a different part of the task.

The first year and the second year passed, and when they were coming towards the end of the third year, the finest branch looked just like Kaguya's order HORAI-no-TAMA-no-EDA was completed. There were many many failed attempts which made a heap in the corner of the workshop.

Kuramochi-no-Miko got on the boat again so that he could pretend he was returning from HORAI with the splendid TAMA-no-EDA in the box.

Look! Master's come back!

Welcome back, Sir!

What's that?

Must be treasure.

I'm visiting Princess Kaguya, not going back home.

At Okina's house...
Kaguya, I've just heard that Mr. Kuramochi will come soon.

You have to decide this time, Got it, Kaguya?

Master, Mr. Kuramochi is here now.

Boiled water was served to tired looking Kuramochi-no-Miko.

I, I got back from HORAI just now. W, Would you show the branch to P, Princess Kaguya, please?

He pretended being out of breath that he was in a hurry.

What a splendid branch! I've never seen such a thing in my life.

Amazingly, the stalk was shining like gold, the leaves looked like jade, the flowers were sparkling crystals and the berries looked like pearls.

Kuramochi-no-Miko began to talk about the HORAI trip. He was sure that Princess Kaguya inside the blinds could hear him.

Soon after setting off to the East-Sea, we were caught in a storm.
We lost our bearings and we were adrift in the sea for hundreds days.
One day, we were almost killed by a monster.
Sometimes, we were forced to eat roots because we had no other food.
Some of us were ill.
We had no help from anyone else during our journey.

One morning, we realized that there was an island.

Let's go closer to that island

Yes, Sir!

We looked around the island for a couple of days.

Then, a young beautiful woman who looked like a celestial nymph came down from the mountain and began to take water with a silver bowl.

Excuse me, could you tell me what this place is called?

Kaguya is more beautiful, though..

This is Mount HORAI.

After all !

Although we tried to chase after her, she disappeared in a blink. It was very rugged there.

t's noisy outside, sn't it? What's that?

Certainly, but it won't be any problem. My wife will take care of it. Go on, please. What did you do after that?

Kuramochi-no-Miko continued his story.

t was so rugged that we walked around the base of the mountain for a couple of days.

Amazingly, we saw incredible trees with beautiful flowers.

Clear water was flowing, which sparkled in gold, silver and purplish blue.

The bridge which crossed the stream was decorated with jewels.

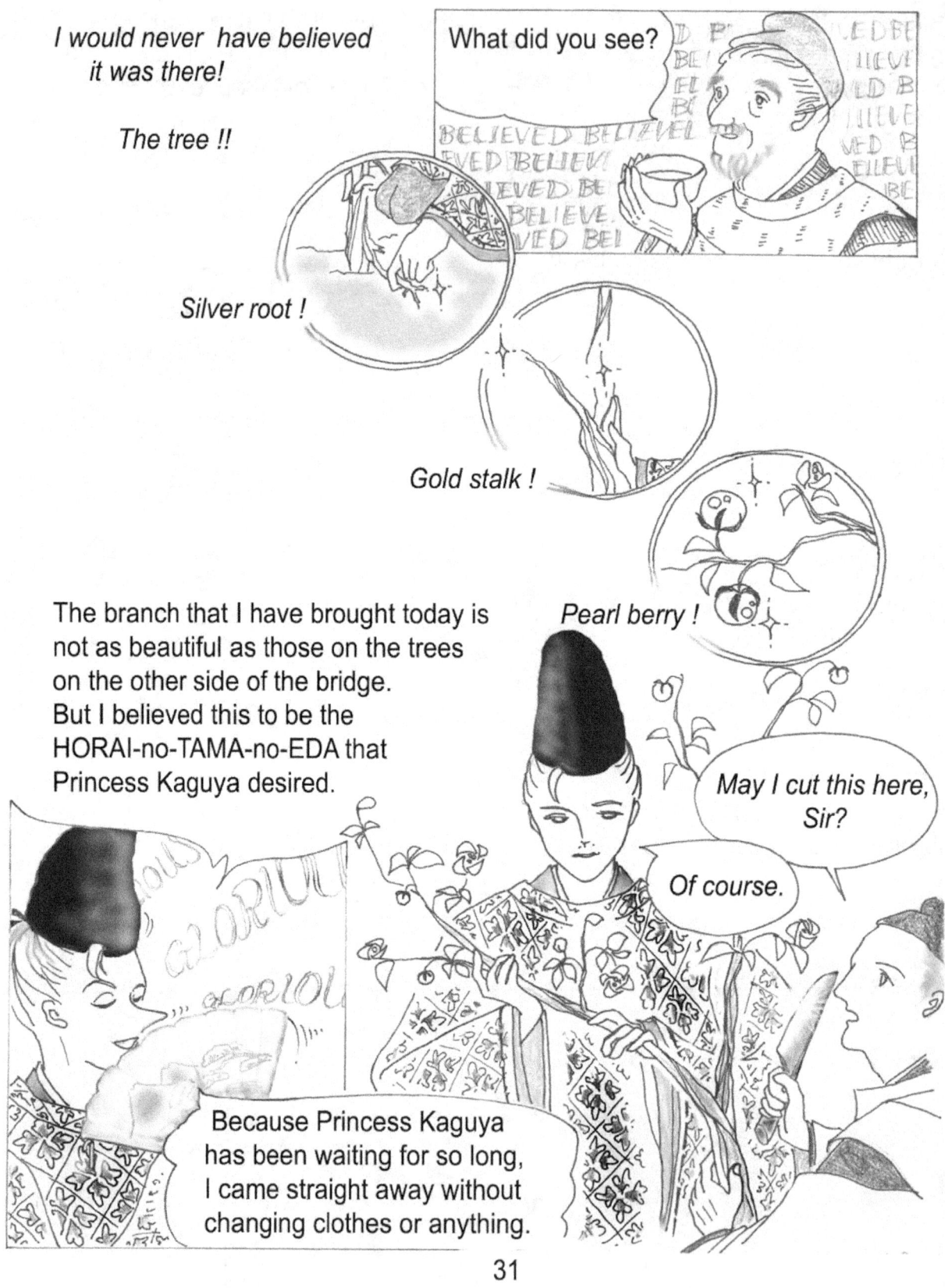

I would never have believed it was there!

The tree !!

What did you see?

Silver root !

Gold stalk !

The branch that I have brought today is not as beautiful as those on the trees on the other side of the bridge. But I believed this to be the HORAI-no-TAMA-no-EDA that Princess Kaguya desired.

Pearl berry !

May I cut this here, Sir?

Of course.

Because Princess Kaguya has been waiting for so long, I came straight away without changing clothes or anything.

31

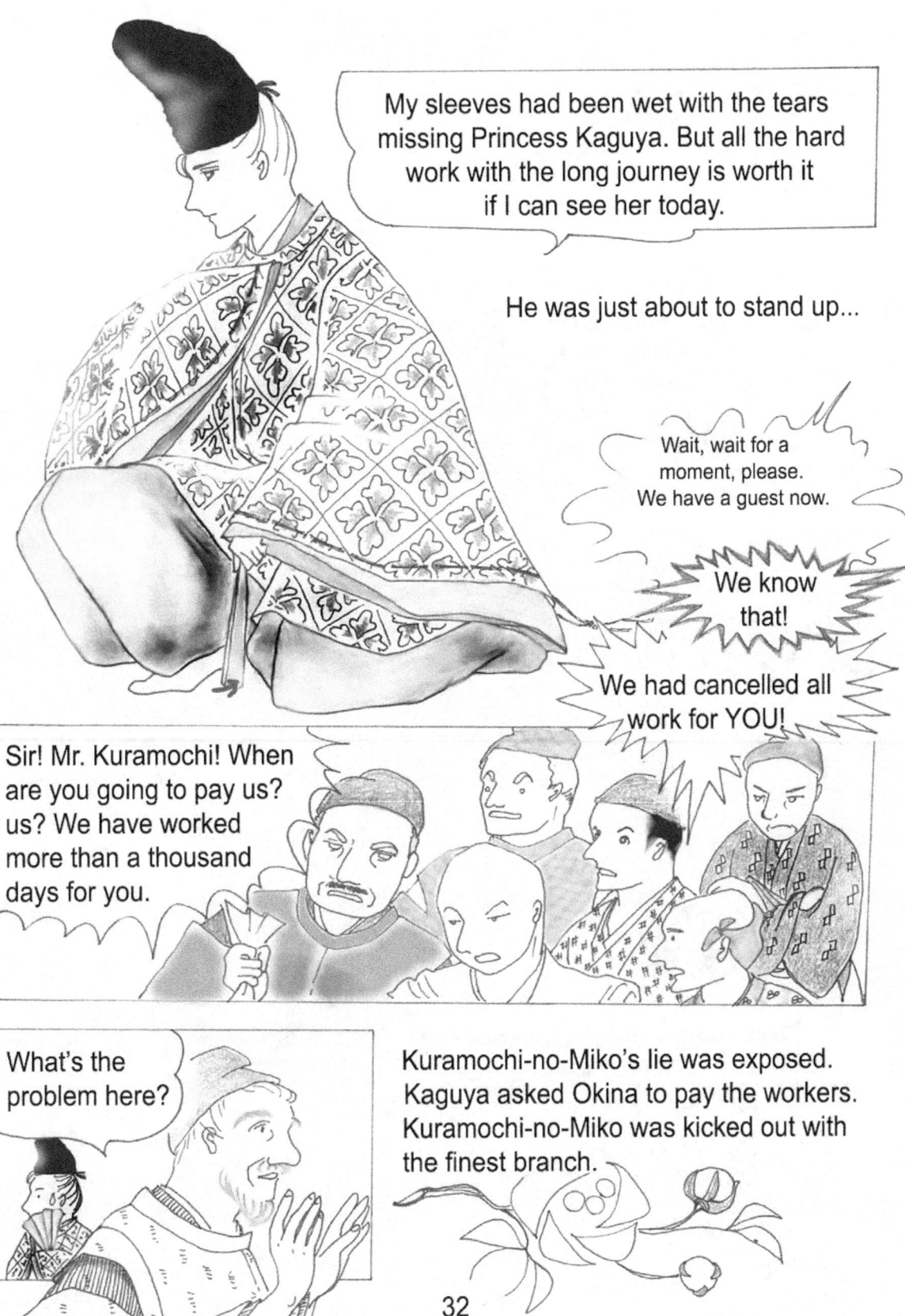

My sleeves had been wet with the tears missing Princess Kaguya. But all the hard work with the long journey is worth it if I can see her today.

He was just about to stand up...

Wait, wait for a moment, please. We have a guest now.

We know that!

We had cancelled all work for YOU!

Sir! Mr. Kuramochi! When are you going to pay us? us? We have worked more than a thousand days for you.

What's the problem here?

Kuramochi-no-Miko's lie was exposed. Kaguya asked Okina to pay the workers. Kuramochi-no-Miko was kicked out with the finest branch.

32

33

Okina was called by the Mikado[11].
Okina visited the Imperial Court.
The rumors of Kaguya's challenge to
the noblemen had reached the Mikado.

How's Princess Kaguya?

She's fine, thank you very much.

By the way...
if she comes here,
I'll promise you that you'll
be given a high rank.
How do you feel
about that?

I really appreciate the offer, but
I cannot force her to say
'Yes'.

"I wonder whether I could see her
on my hunting trip?"

The Mikado turned away from Okina
deep in thought, muttering to himself...

Mikado

34

35

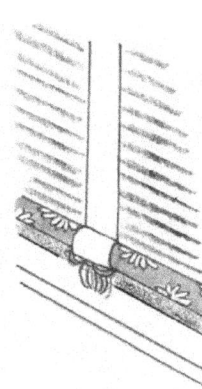

Princess Kaguya hid inside...
All that remained was
an indescribable radiance.
The Mikado could not
concentrate on his work.
All he could think about
was Kaguya's beauty.

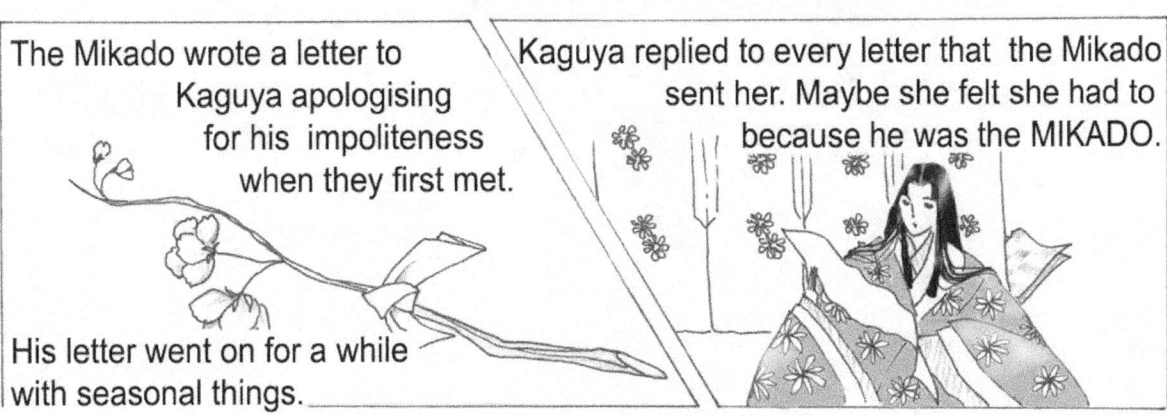

The Mikado wrote a letter to
Kaguya apologising
for his impoliteness
when they first met.

His letter went on for a while
with seasonal things.

Kaguya replied to every letter that the Mikado
sent her. Maybe she felt she had to
because he was the MIKADO.

And
after three more years...

Okina and Ouna began to notice
Kaguya becoming tearful everytime
she looked up at the moon.

Poor Kaguya.

Okina and Ouna could not
do anything to cheer Kaguya
up, except being beside her.

36

Kaguya,
how are you, today?
It hurts to see you like this.

"I have to tell you something.
I belong to the Moon and I was sent to
this planet for a purpose.
But... I have to go back to the Moon on
the night of 15th of August."

What!

"On the evening of the Harvest
Moon, people from the Moon
will be sent here."
Okina and Ouna were
very surprised.

Listen! This is the order of the
Mikado. We have to protect
Princess Kaguya! Send two
thousand soldiers to
Okina's place!

Okina asked the Mikado
to guard Kaguya so that
she would not be taken
away.

37

At midnight, two thousand soldiers guarded
Okina's house. The night was brighter than
the daytime, because of the full Moon.
It was so bright that even people's pores were
visible.

Okina was so furious that
he promised himself that
he would do whatever
it took to save Kaguya,
-going to take their eyes
 with his long finger-nails...
-going to take their hair and
 pull them down to the ground...

It used to be told that people
could become devils easily
when they were in a bad fix.

Suddenly, a burst of light grew and clouds floated down form the sky carrying people on them. They hovered just above the ground and one of them carried a HAGOROMO[12] in her arms.

The bright light from the clouds blinded the guards, who suddenly lost their strength. The heavily bolted doors opened by themselves.

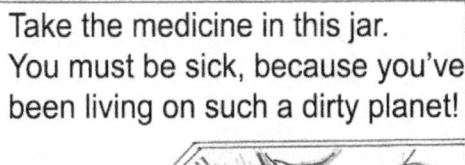
Take the medicine in this jar. You must be sick, because you've been living on such a dirty planet!

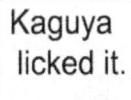
Kaguya licked it.

Princess, please put the HAGOROMO on.

Wait!

Once I put it on, my memories of my time on earth will be gone in an instant. I have something to do before I put it on.

Kaguya picked up a brush and started to write letters. One of them was to Okina and Ouna. She wrote;

" I am leaving my over-garment with you as something by which you can remember me. Please look up at the moon and think of me.
    Thank you very much for bringing me up. "

40

Kaguya left her all grief behind on earth
and went back to the Moon.

Another letter was to the Mikado and was sent with the medicine that Kaguya licked, the Elixir of Life.

Unless I can see Princess Kaguya, this is useless!!

Which mountain is the highest?

It's in SURUGA. It's near here and nearest to Heaven, Sir.

Take the jar and the letter, and burn these at the mountain for me.

Yes, Sir !

The jar containing the 'Elixir of life' and Kaguya's letter were put into the fire at the top of the mountain. It was known as the mountain closest to the heavens.

As many soldiers under arms climbed up this mountain at that time, it named ' Mt. FUJI₁₃ '

FU （富） means WEALTH
JI （士） means SOLDIER
'The mountain has
a wealth of strong soldiers.'

It is said that the smoke is still going up to the heavens.

Ninety years later,
when Mt. FUJI errupted, it was told
that a nymph appeared in the clouds.

43

YUKI-HIME

Present days in 21 Century, at the west side of Mt. HOUEI, you may see Princess KAGUYA on the surface when Mt. FUJI is covered with snow.

(from Home Page 'Fuji City in Shizuoka', Japan)

kyoto

Tokyo

Mt. FUJI

Shizuoka

Osaka

Nara

There is Suruga at the foot of Mt.Fuji.

[**TAKETORI MONOGATARI**] was first told in the early 10th Century and continued to spread by word of mouth. The author is unknown; however, it is the oldest Japanese literature in KANA script. The original book does not exist, however the oldest known copy goes back to the AZUCHI-MOMOYAMA period (TENSHO 1573~1592).

Although it is difficult even for Japanese people to fully understand the depth of the language (it was expressed in the old Japanese language)   used in this story, I have tried to interpret it as simply as possible. It would be wonderful if readers were to be interested in the story and the culture through "Princess Kaguya."

The political background to this story
The period was the heyday of the Aristocratic class. The Emperor was at
the head, his sprawling palace the administrative centre of the empire.
The culture flourished in music, WAKA (short poems) and people enjoyed elegant dancing. They had much knowledge, wisdom and sophistication, their lives were incredibly luxurious - they seemed to spare no expense.
Their political power though, gradually weakened and changed to the Shogunate, the culture which survives to the present day.

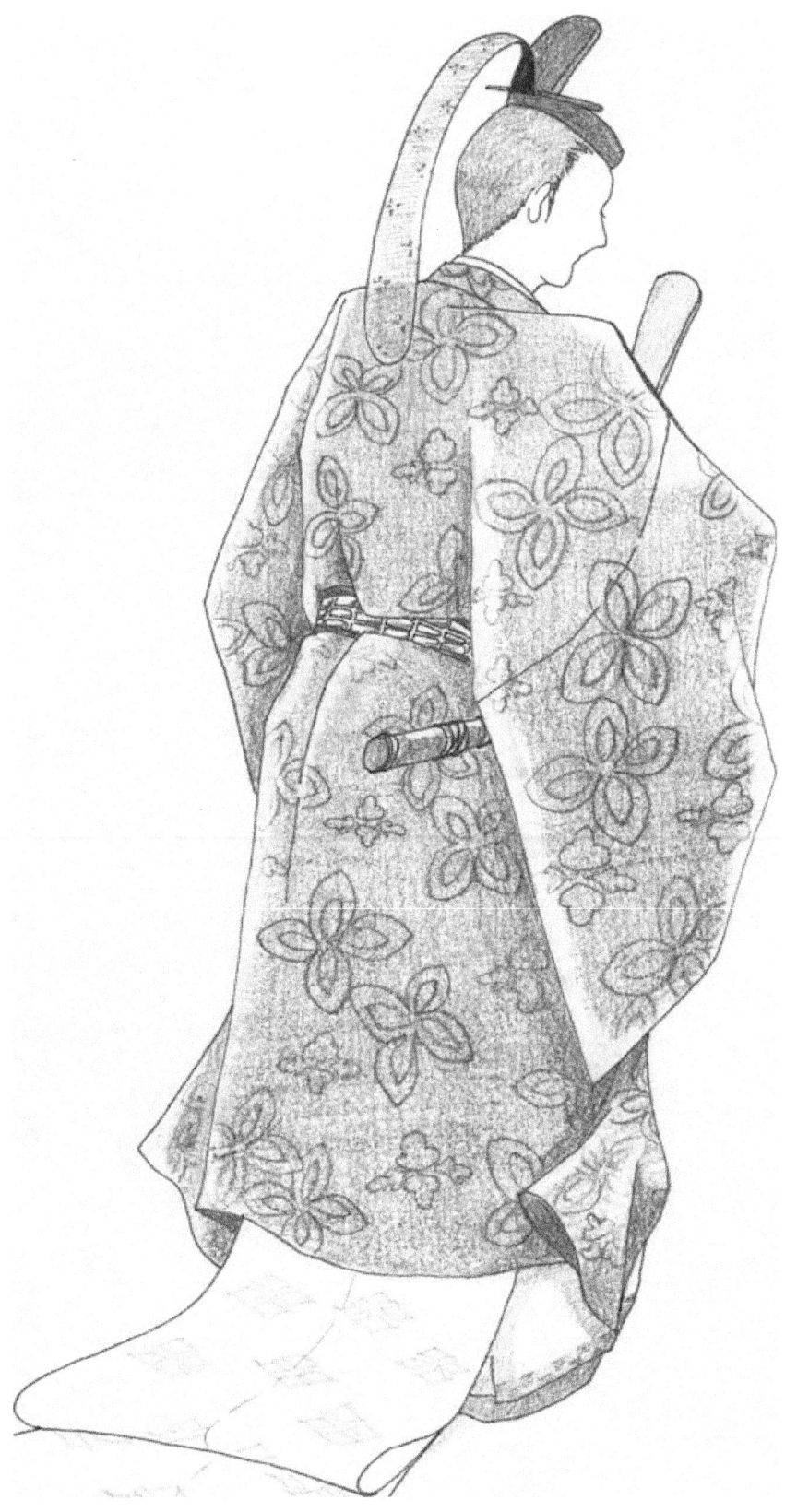

Appendix

1. **Kaguya** : NAYOTAKE- no- KAGUYA HIME (なよ竹のかぐや姫). She is literally referred to as "A beautiful shiny girl like a fresh young bamboo"

2. **Taketori-no-Okina**(竹取の翁): 'Okina' is a pronoun of an old man. 'Taketori-no-Okina' means 'An old man who makes a living with bamboo crafting.'

   In those times, there were no surnames in the working class families. To avoid confusion between people with same names, they took their jobs or a description of the place where they lived and turned it into their surname.

3. **Ouna**(嫗) : It is a pronoun of an old woman.

4. **Miko**(皇子) : A child of Emperor or a posterity of Emperor.

5. Blinds : Formally known as **Misu** （御簾） . In the noble society, when a woman has reached her mid-teens, she had to stay inside the blinds when she talked to any men. She was only to be seen by a man who she was to marry.

6. **HORAI-no-TAMA-no-EDA** (蓬莱の玉の枝)-*A jewel branch in Horai* : Horai was an island known to be a paradise, located somewhere in the East Sea. It was an imaginary island where godly people lived and the island was said to be filled with indescribable wealth.

7. **HOTOKE-no-MIISHI-no-HACHI** (仏の御石の鉢)-*A bowl used by Buddha* : The bowl which Buddha used to receive his alms. Buddha existed around 2500 years ago, he was born in North East India and spread Buddhism around the world.

Buddhism came to Japan with a beautiful statue and a scripture in 552, The Emperor at that time discussed with men of Cabinet rank whether they should have worshiped or not.

A chief priest of a temple

8. TSUBAKURAME-no-KOYASUGAI

(　燕　の子安貝)-*A KOYASUGAI in a swallow's nest* : 'Tsubakurame' is a swallow.

'Koyasugai' is a kind of sea shell, which was given to pregnant woman as a charm for a safe delivery.　Although there was no actual link between swallows and shells, in those days the shells were often found in their broken nests.

KOYASUGAI : A kind of rolled shell. It lives in warm
sea. Length is about 8cm.
Skin is thick and strong, one side is inflated like an egg.

9. **RYU-no-KUBI-no-TAMA** (竜の首の玉)-*A jewel at the neck of a Dragon* : Ryu (Dragon) was known to be living deep in the sea, however, in some stories, they appeared high above the sky. Its jewel is said to control the powers of nature.

10. **HINEZUMI-no-KAWAGINU** (火鼠の皮衣)-*A jacket made with the fur of HNEZUMI* : Hinezumi was supposed to live in a volcano. A garment made with the fur, it was told, could not be burnt. HINEZUMI is supposed to be a kind of weasel.

11. **Mikado**(帝) : The Emperor of Japan.

12.**HAGOROMO**(羽衣)：It is a shawl. It is told that Celestial Nymphs wear them and they are able to fly with them.

13. **FUJI** (富士): There is another theory for naming 'FUJI'. The thing Mikado ordered to burn was the 'Elixir of life', which gives immortality. (不死)." For expressing the meaning, people used other KANJI characters. It is also pronounced [fuji].

Few years after the story of Princess Kaguya,
how were five men?
An old tradition says that…

Ishitsukuri-no-Miko was ordered to be a correspondent to China and came back safely few years later. When he died, he was at quite high rank - that was 6th from the top.

Abe-no-Miushi had lost his nerve for a while and he was so careless with the wealth given by his father. He spent rest of his life peacefully, and he died 30 years later.

Isonokami-no-Marotari took years to recover. When he became better, no one remembered him. His late life seemed not so good.

Ohtomo-no-Miyuki was sent away on a task by the Emperor. He was so successful, and he died at age 67 after coming back.

Kuramochi-no-Miko had been spiritless for a while, he disappeared suddenly. 10 years later he was found in a forest and was brought back to his house.

Although he eventually became a member of the cabinet, he had been refusing the promotion since then No one knew the reason why. He and his four brothers died after prolonged illness 30 years later.

It has long been known that bamboo flowering was extremely rare. You can only witness the flowers of a single bamboo once in 60 to 100 years. Therefore a superstition was born in Japan that when a bamboo flower came out, there will be a change in the flow of time. In the story of Princess Kaguya, it was a mystery that a girl appeared in a bamboo tree. Later, she grew up to change the lives of many people - even including the life of the Emperor. Maybe if you see a bamboo flower somewhere, something significant may change in your life too.

Eiko Jasmine

Additional notes on the time period of Princess Kaguya

with illustrations

KICHOU (几帳)

A kind of blind. It was used as the screen.
The objects for ladies on the table ; A pot for hair oil and an item for burning incense

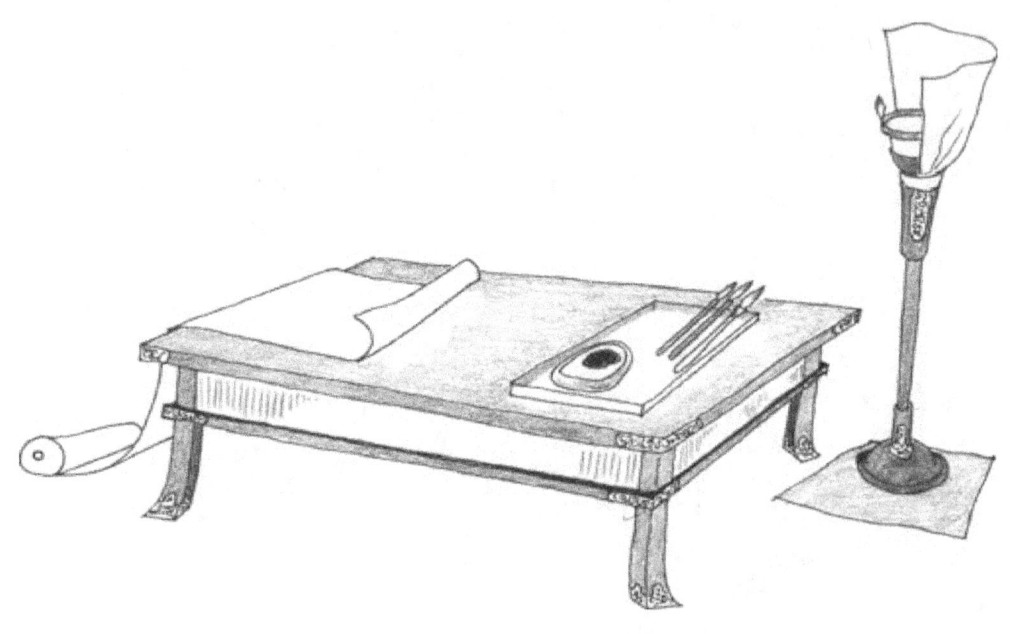

FUZUKUE(文机)：Writing desk

GISSHA(牛車)

A carriage which a noble person used when he or she wanted to go out

NYOKAN(女官) : A court lady

KEMARI (蹴鞠) :

A kind of sport in the imperial garden for men.
They enjoyed a game of kicking a ball up in the air.

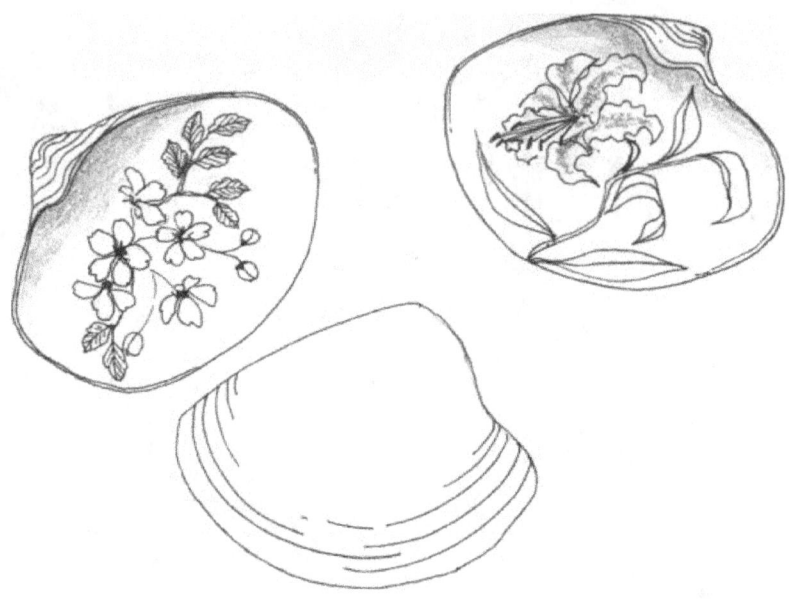

KAIAWASE(貝合)

A kind of play for women and children. They enjoyed matching shells.
Each shell was painted with a beautiful picture in gold.

GAGAKU (雅楽)

Playing musical instruments

MAI (舞)

Elegant dance was a symbol of noble society.

The game of 'GO' (碁)

People enjoyed the game with small black pebbles and white ones on the board which is like a chess board.

FUNA ASOBI (船遊び)

In the season of flowers people enjoyed boating.

SAKURA (桜)

Cherry blossom : It is the national tree of Japan.
It is loved and people enjoy the sight of it in Spring.

KIKU (菊)

Chrysanthemum : It is the National flower of Japan.
Any kind of chrysanthemums have been shown in Autumn in Japan.
The emblem of the Emperor of Japan is the chrysanthemum.

IKE　(池)

Most big gardens have a pond in Japan.

TSUKIMI (月見)

Even today, in the Autumn people gaze at the Full Moon and enjoy.
And they may think of Princess Kaguya.

FOLLOWERS to HUNT

They are ready to follow the Master.

IMPERIAL COURT

At the period of this story The Imperial Court was in a sprawling mass of buildings for the administrative organ.

Play

Children played with bamboo. They likened it to a horse.

References

Taketori monogatari　竹取物語（日本古典文学全集）

Yamato Tsukikage- sho　大和月影抄（平沼兵庫氏　筆）

Graphic Wide REKISHI　グラフィックワイド歴史（東京法令出版株式会社）

KOKUGO BINRAN　国語便覧　（浜島書店）

KOUSAIJI temple Home page　（広済寺）

Fuji City in Shizuoka Home page

About the Author...

Eiko Jasmine

Eiko Jasmine was born in Japan in 1955. She was formally trained
and worked as a teacher in Japan for several years and has
extensive experience in teaching English and Japanese as parts of
the curriculum. After moving to the UK, she continued to teach
Japanese literature at Japanese School in Shropshire for 10 years,
before becoming the headmistress of the North East of England
Japanese School in Tyne & Wear. She had been introducing
Japanese culture to people during her time in the UK.